What is Stress?

Dealing with Stress

Dwayne Booker

S☺CiAL AND EM☺Ti☺NAL LEARNiNG
FOR THE **REAL** WORLD™

Rosen Classroom™

Do you ever feel scared?
Do you ever feel nervous?

Do you worry about school?
Do you worry about your family?

That is called stress.
Everyone feels stress sometimes.

Stress might make your body
feel bad.
What does it feel like?

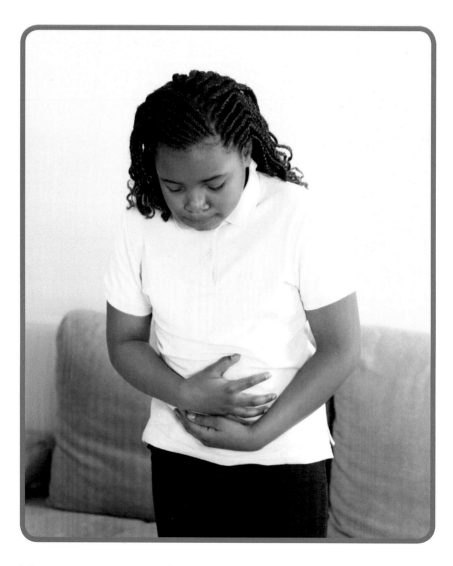

Your stomach might hurt.
You might not want to eat.

Your head might hurt.
You might not be able to sleep.

How can you feel better?
First, take a deep breath.

Go on a walk.
Do something that makes
you happy.

Talk to someone.
Tell them your worries.

Stress is a part of life.
Use your skills when you
feel stress!

Words to Know

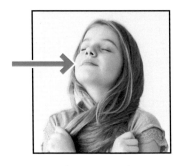

breath

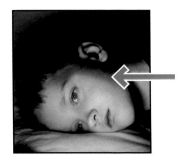

head

walk